©1999 Editions La Joie de lire SA
Originally published under the title
Le Nöel de Milton
by La Joie de lire SA,
2 bis, rue Saint-Léger, CH-1205 Genève
English Text © 2000 Chronicle Books LLC.
All rights reserved.

Book design by Haydé Ardalan
and Kristine Brogno.
Typeset in Blue Century.
Printed in China.

ISBN 0-8118-2842-5
Library of Congress Cataloging-in-
Publication Data Available

Distributed in Canada by Raincoast Books
9050 Shaughnessy Street
Vancouver, British Columbia V6P 6E5

10 9 8 7 6 5 4 3 2 1

Chronicle Books LLC
85 Second Street
San Francisco, California 94105

www.chroniclebooks.com

Milton's Christmas

by Haydé Ardalan

chronicle books · san francisco

What a perfect Christmas morning.

I think I'll stay inside.

I'm going to catch that bird!

Ouch.

Those pine needles are sharp.

A present for me?
What could it be?

I don't save wrapping paper.

Eek! A mouse!

Forget about the mouse.
What do we have here?

Shrimp, my favorite!

The holidays can be so tiring.

Time to sleep... to dream...

Oh no,
a nightmare!

Uh oh.
Somebody made a big mess.

Maybe this would be a good time for me to go outside.

Merry Christmas!

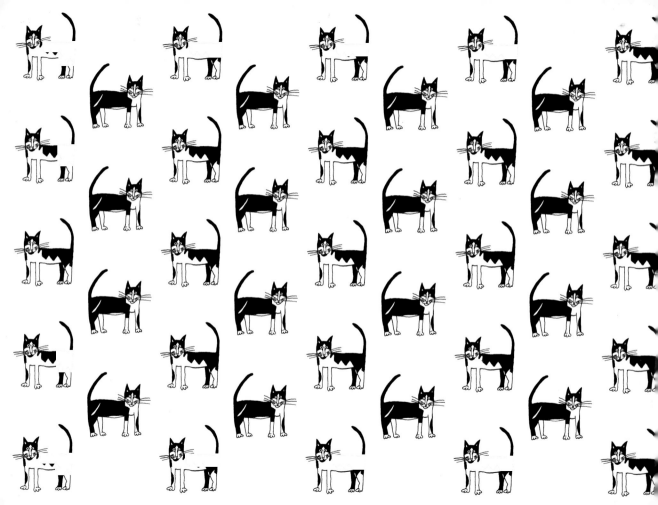